Tim hunted through the little drawers

Tim
Minds the Shop
by
Ella Monckton

Illustrated by
Patricia W. Turner

F. Warne & Co. Ltd.   London & New York

To Timothy Webb

7232 0972 3
PRINTED IN GREAT BRITAIN

Tim Minds the Shop

MR. AND MRS. WATER-RAT kept a small General shop on the banks of a stream. The front door and the shop window were just above high water mark, and there was a flight of pebble steps leading down to the landing stage where Mr. Water-Rat moored his boat.

This was a most useful arrangement for those of his regular customers who spent most of their time on the stream.

For those who lived on the land, there was a back door at the top of the bank. It was well screened by hazelnut bushes, and led into a passage leading to the shop.

Both doors were open in the day time and Mr. Water-Rat shut and bolted them at closing time.

The shop itself was always clean and tidy with a counter at each end. Behind them were shelves, and rows of little drawers with wooden knobs to pull them out. The walls were whitewashed and the floor was made of flat well-scrubbed stones.

Mr. Water-Rat stood at one counter where groceries were sold, and Mrs. Water-Rat sat with her knitting behind the other counter and sold everything else from acorn cups and saucers, to sheep's wool for knitting baby clothes, and the finest cob-webs by the yard.

The shop itself was always clean and tidy

7

Mr. and Mrs. Water-Rat were proud of their shop; almost as proud as they were of their two children, Tim and Fluff.

Fluff was still only a baby, and spent most of the time in a cradle of plaited grass.

But Tim was nearly full grown, and thought quite a lot of himself.

After school he helped his father serve in the shop, or took a basket of goods round to someone who was ill or too old to come to the shop.

One fine spring day when the daffodils were about to bloom, Mrs. Water-Rat thought it would be nice to go downstream to visit her sister and

show her how well Fluff had grown during the winter.

Mr. Water-Rat could take her in his boat, and leave Tim to mind the shop.

At first Mr. Water-Rat was very doubtful.

"Tim has never been left all alone before," he said. "Think of all the things he might do wrong."

"Nonsense," said Mrs. Water-Rat. "He is quite old enough to manage for a few hours. It is high time he started learning the business so that you and I can take a day off now and then. If we leave directly after dinner we shall be back before it begins to grow dark."

Tim was delighted at the idea.

He had thought for some time that he could manage everything as well as his father and possibly even a little better.

Mr. Water-Rat took some persuading, but in the end he agreed. During the morning he gave Tim a great many instructions, most of which went in at one ear and out of the other. (Like all young water rats, Tim's ears were small and round and set very close to his head.)

So after an early dinner, Mrs. Water-Rat washed up the dishes, hung the dish-cloth up to dry, and took off her apron. Then she tied a spotted handkerchief over her head and wrapped Fluff in her best shawl.

Mr. Water-Rat put on his mackintosh and went down the front steps to the landing stage. He pulled the boat closer and arranged some cushions on the seats.

Tim helped his mother to carry Fluff and a basket of choice groceries down the steps. When they were all settled in the boat Mr. Water-Rat said, "Remember Tim, be polite to the customers, and keep the till locked. You may eat as many bulls-eyes as you like, and three chocolate bars from the white box on the bottom shelf."

Then he dipped his oars and rowed smartly down-stream. Tim went back up the steps into the shop, put on his father's big white apron and waited for his first customer.

Unluckily for him it was Mrs. Hedgehog. She was always a prickly person and to-day she was particularly short-tempered.

"Good morning, Tim. Where's your father?" she asked.

Tim explained that both his father and his mother were away for the afternoon. Mrs. Hedgehog sniffed.

"Well, give me half-a-pound of bacon, a pound of brown sugar, and an ounce of mixed herbs," she said. "And I am in a hurry."

"Certainly madam," said Tim politely.

Mrs. Hedgehog sat down on a chair by the counter

and stared at him with her beady black eyes. This made Tim so nervous that he cut the bacon too thickly and weighed out the wrong kind of sugar. When he had put that right he looked for the mixed herbs and just could not find them. He pulled out one drawer after another while Mrs. Hedgehog grunted with impatience and drummed on the counter with her stubby little fingers.

Tim pulled a drawer out too far and a shower of pepper-corns went rattling and bouncing all over the floor.

Mrs. Hedgehog got up, put the bacon and sugar into her basket, and counted out some money on to the counter.

"I can't wait all day," she said crossly, and waddled out of the shop.

After she had gone Tim found a new packet of mixed herbs on the shelf right in front of his nose!

It was too late to call Mrs. Hedgehog back so he went down on his hands and knees to scoop up the peppercorns, and put them back into the correct drawer.

He was still down on the floor when he heard a patter of feet and a lot of shrill squeaking. Getting up quickly he bumped his head hard on the edge of the counter.

Two small green frogs who had just come into the

shop from the stream, looked at him and giggled delightedly.

Tim forgot his father's advice and asked them quite crossly what they wanted.

Between bursts of laughter they said that they had two pennies to buy sweets.

They took a long time to make up their minds which kind to choose and Tim had taken down nearly every jar from the shelf, before they decided to have a half-pennyworth of four different kinds.

While Tim was weighing them out and putting them into small paper bags, they chased each other round the shop covering the clean floor with little muddy footprints.

Tim caught them, banged their heads together, and they rushed out clutching their sweets and squealing at the tops of their voices.

Only when he heard the plop they made going back into the stream did he notice that they had

They looked at him and giggled delightedly

16

not given him the money for the sweets. He put two pennies of his own into the till, shut it with a bang, and put the sweet jars back on the lowest shelf.

He had only just finished when Mr. Mole came in to buy a button to match the three already on his waistcoat. With him was Mrs. Mouse to inquire if the knitting wool she had ordered was in yet. She sat

quietly on the customer's chair while Tim hunted through the little drawers on his mother's side of the shop.

He found almost every kind of button except the kind that matched Mr. Mole's other three, which were round and flat and shiny.

"I always get them here," said Mr. Mole. "I particularly want one to-day because I am going out to tea."

"I think Tim," said Mrs. Mouse in her gentle voice, "that your mother keeps Mr. Mole's buttons in a white box in the left hand corner of the bottom shelf."

Tim gave her a grateful look as he found the box which was indeed full of round flat shiny buttons.

When Mr. Mole had gone, Mrs. Mouse got up and said kindly, "Don't bother about my wool now, Tim. I've got two other calls to make and I'll look in on my way home. That will give you time to have a look for it. Is this the first time you have minded the shop by yourself?"

"Yes," said Tim. "And so far I haven't been very good at it."

He told Mrs. Mouse about Mrs. Hedgehog and the cheeky frogs.

"You live and learn," said Mrs. Mouse cheerfully and pattered up the passage to the back door of the shop.

After she had gone Tim had no more customers for a long time.

He began to feel rather bored until he remembered the chocolate bars. He took the box off the shelf and opened it on the counter. He took one out, peeled off the silver paper and went to the front door of the shop.

He thought that it would help to pass the time if he ate it very slowly, sitting on the doorstep and watching the stream flow by.

It really was a lovely day

20

It really was a lovely day. The sky was pale blue with big white clouds sweeping across it, so that the sun went in and out and the shadows chased each other over the fields.

The stream ran chuckling between it's banks, so clear and shallow that Tim could see the small fish flicking about just above the pebbles.

It was a perfect day to go fishing, or hunting, or just looking for things.

Then a small boat came shooting upstream and stopped by the pebble steps. In the boat was a young water rat named Joe. He was the son of Mr. Water-Rat's best customer, and Tim did not like him very much because he gave himself airs and had a boat of his own.

Tim went quickly back into the shop and stood beside the grocery counter. Joe swaggered in and looked round.

He was carrying an empty bottle.

"Hullo, Tim.   Where's your father?" he asked.
"Mum wants some vinegar."

Tim explained that both his parents were away for
the afternoon and that he was in charge of the shop.
"I'll fill your bottle for you," he finished.

Joe handed over the bottle and Tim took it to the

corner of the shop where there were two little barrels on stands with taps in them. He was so sure that the right hand one held vinegar that he had half filled the bottle before he found that it was paraffin.

"Oh bother!" he said, and quickly turned off the tap.

Joe who was close behind him, sniffed and then roared with laughter. "You're a fine shopkeeper," he jeered. "Now what do you do? You can't put vinegar into a paraffiny bottle!"

"I'll get another one," Tim muttered, feeling very hot and upset at his silly mistake. He went quickly out of the shop and into Mrs. Water-Rat's tidy little kitchen, where it took him some time to find a clean empty bottle.

When he went back into the shop there was no sign of Joe. And it did not take him long to notice that the white box, which he had left on the counter, had gone too.

It took him some time to find a bottle

24

Tim was really angry. First the little frogs had cheated him of twopence, and now Joe had run off with a whole box of chocolate bars.

He rushed out of the shop and down the steps, and was just in time to see Joe's boat leaving the landing stage.

He shouted, but Joe took no notice.

Without pausing to think, Tim plunged into the stream and gave chase.

25

He was a strong swimmer, and about half a mile downstream he caught up with the boat.

He took hold of one side and hung on grimly while Joe tried to hit him with an oar.

After a short struggle the boat tipped over, and Joe, together with the box of chocolate bars, fell into the water . . . .

Tim and Joe swam ashore, the little boat floated upside down until it was caught in some rushes, and the box of chocolate bars settled quietly down at the bottom of the stream.

"Now what did you want to do that for?" asked Joe sulkily as he squeezed the water out of his coat.

"You took that box off the counter while I was out of the shop," said Tim angrily. "That makes you a thief."

"I'm not," said Joe indignantly. "It all goes down to Father's account. It was your fault for putting paraffin into my vinegar bottle. You were such ages finding another that I couldn't wait, so I helped myself."

Tim could not think of a suitable reply to this, so he turned his back and began to walk along the bank.

Joe ran after him. "All right, I'm sorry," he said. "Please help me to bale out my boat, and I'll row you home."

"I ought to go back at once," said Tim, suddenly remembering that he had left the shop with no one to mind it.

"It won't take a minute to help me," pleaded Joe. "And it will be much quicker in the end to row home."

Tim agreed, chiefly because he hated walking so much.

But it took quite a long time to disentangle the boat from the rushes and empty it out, and longer still to find the oars which had floated some way further downstream. Then they had to row back against the current.

Tim grew more and more anxious as time went on, and he grew more positive that he should never have left the shop with both doors open and no one to serve customers who might come.

When at last they reached the landing stage he jumped out, and without a word to Joe, he ran as fast as he could up the steps and into the shop.

What a sight it was!

Drawers had been pulled out and their contents scattered on the floor; sweet jars lay on their sides half empty; the tap of the vinegar barrel had been turned on and a stream of vinegar was spreading in pools

across the floor. And worst of all the drawer of the till stood open and empty because he had forgotten to lock it.

Tim took one look and began to howl at the top of his voice. He could not stop even when Joe came running up the steps to discover what the noise was about.

"Well here's a go," he said looking round him in amazement.

"And it's all your fault," shouted Tim. "If you hadn't taken that chocolate I should not have left the shop. What *will* Father say?"

Now Joe was not really bad at heart. He looked at the mess again and felt truly sorry for his share in the disaster.

"I'm sorry Tim," he said. "Stop crying, and I'll help you clear up."

Tim rubbed his eyes with his paw.

The more he looked at it the more hopeless it seemed that they could ever sort out and put back the terrible mixture of split peas and tea and currants and rice and other groceries which lay scattered over the floor.

He was sure that half the sweets had gone from the upturned jars, and there had been at least five shillings in the now empty till.

" *Oh dear!   Whatever shall I do?* "

He was about to say so, when little Mrs. Mouse came pattering down the passage. She stopped in the back doorway and stared.

"Mercy me!" she cried. "Whatever has been going on here?"

"Oh, Mrs. Mouse!" wailed Tim. "I left the shop to chase Joe and when I got back someone had been in and overturned everything. Oh dear! Whatever shall I do?"

"Humph," said Mrs. Mouse. "Who knew that you were here by yourself?"

"Mrs. Hedgehog, but she would never do such a dreadful thing. And Mr. Mole and you, but you wouldn't do it either," said Tim. He thought for a moment. "Oh, yes. Two young frogs came in to buy sweets and I smacked them for making foot marks on the clean floor."

"Well there you are," cried Joe. "They must have been watching from the rushes and saw you follow me.

Look! Only the bottom shelves and the drawers were touched because they couldn't reach any higher. I know where they hide. We'll go after them."

"I can't leave things like this," cried Tim, looking despairingly at the state of the shop. "Mother and Father might come back before I return."

Mrs. Mouse began to roll up her sleeves.

"Now Tim," she said briskly, "find me one of your mother's aprons and show me where she keeps her broom and pail, and brush and dustpan. Then you and Joe look for those naughty frogs and recover the money that was in the till. I expect they will have eaten all the sweets by now, but that can't be helped.

"Now hurry or your mother and father really will be back."

"Yes, hurry," urged Joe.

Tim gave Mrs. Mouse a very grateful look and the two young water rats ran out of the shop.

Directly they had gone Mrs. Mouse set to work.
First she mopped up the spilt vinegar. Then she put
the jars back on the shelves. Then with her quick
little paws she sorted out the peas and the rice and the
currants and the nutmegs and the peppercorns and all
the other things, and put them back into their right
drawers. She swept up the salt, the flour and the sugar,
and she scrubbed the floor. All the time she hummed
a little song to herself.

He stopped and put his finger to his lips

Meanwhile Joe led the way along the bank.

When they had gone a short distance he stopped and put his finger to his lips.

Tim stood quite still and listened.

He could hear some faint squeaks coming from a thick bed of rushes which grew half in and half out of the water.

"They're in there," whispered Joe. "There are about a dozen of them and they think they're pirates. But they are easily frightened. Now you stay here while I creep round to the other side. When I whistle, you give a terrible yell and dash into the rushes. I'll jump in on the other side."

"Right," whispered Tim.

Joe slipped silently away through the grass. After a time Tim heard a soft whistle.

He took a deep breath, gave the most terrible yell he could manage, and then crashed heavily into the rushes.

He landed with a squelch into a shallow pool, and for a moment he thought that the whole world was made of small frogs. They jumped in all directions from under him, over him and around him. Then there was another yell and Joe bounced on top of him, knocking all his breath from his body.

By the time that Tim and Joe had disentangled themselves, there was not a frog to be seen.

They sat up and looked round. On a dry tussock just behind them was a packet of chocolate, a heap of wrapped toffee, a sticky wedge of boiled sweets and three pennies.

"They were dividing the loot," said Joe. "If we search the whole patch perhaps we shall find everything."

For half an hour they searched, putting the things they found in a heap on the dry tussock.

Joe gave a cry of triumph when he discovered half-a-crown in an empty cocoa tin, and a few minutes later Tim came upon three sixpences in a screwed-up paper bag.

When at last there seemed nothing more to find, Tim put the money into his pocket while Joe spread out his coat and made a bundle of all the sweets which had not been spoiled.

Joe gave a cry of triumph

39

Tim agreed that things might have been worse as they walked back along the bank. But he did not believe that even Mrs. Mouse could have cleared up the awful mess in the shop.

But she had. When they walked through the front door everything was clean and tidy and orderly again, and Mrs. Mouse was sitting calmly by the counter

drinking a cup of tea. True, the sweet jars were not quite so full as they had been, the vinegar barrel was nearly empty and some of the flour and sugar had had to be thrown away, but when Tim had put the money back into the till and locked it, and Joe had returned the chocolate and the toffees to their right places, no one would know at a glance that anything had happened.

Tim thanked Mrs. Mouse and promised that if ever she wanted her groceries delivered he would be only too pleased to do it.

She hurried off up the passage, and Tim told Joe that he would really much rather he went home before Mr. and Mrs. Water-Rat came back.

And just how angry was Mr. Water-Rat when Tim told the whole sad story?

Well to begin with he said that it was only what he had expected and proved that Tim was too young to be left in charge of the shop.

Mrs. Water-Rat said that after all it was not Tim's fault entirely and it was high time that the police did something about those young frogs.

In the end, after he had had his supper, Mr. Water-Rat agreed that if the loss of some sweets, flour and sugar, and a quart or so of vinegar had taught Tim some sense it was cheap at the price.

And really it was not so very long after this that the

day came when Mr. and Mrs. Water-Rat again went off for the afternoon and left Tim to mind the shop.

He was very polite to the customers, remembered to lock the till and not for one moment did he set even a foot outside the front door.

Printed by Henry Stone & Son (Printers) Ltd., Banbury.

Printed by Henry Stone & Son (Printers) Ltd., Banbury.
1026.268